**ELMWOOD PARK PUBLIC LIBRARY**
1 CONTI PARKWAY
ELMWOOD PARK, IL 60707
(708) 453-7645

1. A fine is charged for each day a book is kept beyond the due date. The Library Board may take legal action if books are not returned within three months.
2. Books damaged beyond reasonable wear shall be paid for.
3. Each borrower is responsible for all books charged on this card and for all fines accruing on the same.

# Puppy Mudge
# Loves His Blanket

## By Cynthia Rylant

## Illustrated by Isidre Mones

## in the style of Suçie Stevenson

READY-TO-READ

ALADDIN

New York   London   Toronto   Sydney

ALADDIN PAPERBACKS
An imprint of Simon & Schuster Children's Publishing Division
1230 Avenue of the Americas, New York, NY 10020
Text copyright © 2004 by Cynthia Rylant
Illustrations copyright © 2004 by Suçie Stevenson
All rights reserved, including the right of reproduction in whole or in
part in any form.
ALADDIN PAPERBACKS, READY-TO-READ, and colophon are
registered trademarks of Simon & Schuster, Inc.
Also available in a Simon & Schuster Books for Young Readers edition.
Designed by Mark Siegel
The text of this book was set in Goudy.
The illustrations were rendered in pen-and-ink and watercolor.
Manufactured in the United States of America
First Aladdin Paperbacks edition July 2005
10 9 8 7 6 5 4 3 2 1
The Library of Congress Control Number 2004115505
ISBN 0-689-83983-9 (hc.)
ISBN 1-4169-0336-4 (pbk.)

This is Mudge.

He is Henry's puppy.

# Mudge has a blanket.

Mudge LOVES his blanket.

He sleeps on it.

He hides under it.

# He takes it places.

Sometimes he loses it.

# Where is Mudge's blanket now?

# Henry looks on the chair.

Mudge looks on the chair.
No blanket.

Henry looks under the bed.
Mudge looks under the bed.

No blanket.

Mudge is so sleepy.
He needs his blanket.

Mudge sniffs.

He sniffs and sniffs and sniffs.

Good Mudge!
He sniffed all the way . . .

to his blanket!

Now he can rest.